This project is sponsored by

Funded by Proposition 10

Modern Curriculum Press
BEGINNING
TO
READ
Series

What Is It?

Margaret Hillert

Illustrated by Kinuko Craft

ISBN: 0-8136-5556-0
Printed in the United States of America

24 25 26 27 28 29 30   06 05 04 03 02

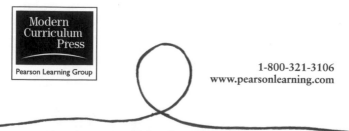

Modern
Curriculum
Press

Pearson Learning Group

1-800-321-3106
www.pearsonlearning.com

What is it? What is it?
Oh, what do I see?
Something little and red.
Go get it for me.

Can you guess what it is?
Can you get it? Oh, no.

For look at it. Look at it.
Look at it go!

But where is it now?
And what will it do?

I see it. I see it.
Do you see it, too?

My little dog helps us.
He likes to have fun.

He can play. He can jump.
He can run, run, run.

I guess it is here.
It is here in this spot.

And now we will get it.
Oh, no, we will not!

And look at it now.
Here it is, where we play.

This little red something
Will not get away.

Now where will it go?
And what can we do?

I see it. I see it.
I see Mother, too.

Down, down it can go.
Down, down it can run.

We like this. We like this.
We like to have fun.

It is fun to play here.
Jump in. One, two, three.

I see it. Go get it.
Go get it for me.

Look here, now. Look here, now.
Look here at this car.

And guess what we see now?
We see where you are.

We see you. We see you.
Oh, you are the one!

Come play with us now.
We can play and have fun.

27

What Is It?

Uses of This Book: Reading for fun. This easy-to-read mystery in verse is sure to excite the rich imaginations of children.

Word List

All of the 55 words used in *What Is It?* are listed. Regular verb forms of words already on the list are not listed separately, but the endings are given in parentheses after the word. Numbers refer to the page on which each word first appears.

7	what		me		help(s)	15	we
	is	8	can		us		not
	it		you		he	17	away
	oh		guess		like(s)	19	mother
	do		no		to	20	down
	I	9	look		have	22	one
	see		at		fun		two
	something	10	but	13	play		three
	little		where		jump	24	car
	and		now		run	25	are
	red		will	14	here	26	the
	go	11	too		in	27	come
	get	12	my		this		with
	for		dog		spot